A

a collection of
short stories

Written by Drake, The Duck Muse
As told to: Diana Kathryn Plopa

Grey Wolfe Publishing, LLC
145 East Fourteen Mile Road
www.GreyWolfePublishing.com

Published by Write Duck Press; an imprint of
Grey Wolfe Publishing, LLC
www.GreyWolfePublishing.com

Print ISBN: 978-1-628282061
E-book ISBN: 978-1-628282054
Library of Congress Control Number: 2018905328

Dedication:

For Zachary:
The first to believe that a Duck Muse could be real.

For Kalli:
The second to believe and never question.

For Dave:
The one who is always supportive of the long hours spent at the keyboard when he'd rather be in a canoe.

Acknowledgements:

Thank you to The Grey Wolfe Writing Pack.
It is because of you that we have been able to come this far, and type this much. Thank you for your continuous support and forever belief in the creative process.

Special Thanks:

To Donald Levin for his friendship and belief that our writing in short form could be a possibility; and especially for his editorial expertise.

About Drake, The Duck Muse

Writers the world over will tell you that they follow their Muse when they create. For some, that means staying connected to the mechanics of storytelling. For others, it means aspiring to tap into some near-spiritual energy that leads one to write words that are worthy of reading. For others still, it means emulating the work of famous writers who've "done it right".

For me, following the Muse means holding courage. Drake, a little invisible Mallard Duck with orange feet and bright blue tints in his feathers, represents my determination to reach beyond myself and tap into the stories that live in my world every day, without fear of people thinking I'm nuts.

Storytelling is a pursuit that often takes me outside of myself. It can be a bit startling and intimidating sometimes. Yet with Drake sitting on my shoulder, I feel I have a partner in this odd journey, and the isolation of seeing the world differently from nearly everyone else around me disappears. With Drake, I can find the courage to take ownership of my creativity and allow self-doubt to take a backseat, as I swim deep into the pond of creation.

I thought the best way to honor that process was to give Drake the lead with this book. So often, story ideas materialize out of thin air. I can't rationally explain where they come from or how I'm able to convey them. There have even been days that I've spent time writing, then look at the results and honestly don't remember how I came to the words. I know there is something inside me that makes it all work. I've named that something, Drake.

Why is Drake a Duck, you ask? Well, when I was younger, the voice of my creativity wasn't always very clear. Sometimes it sounded like a voice under water. At seven, it seemed logical that the voice was a Duck, talking to me while diving for food in the pond. Since that time, Drake and I have, and do, talk often.

Regardless of whether you believe in the notion of a Muse, or the idea that there is an inner voice that speaks to creative people, leading them to do the work, the concept is very real to me.

So, this book is my Thank You to Drake. I wanted to acknowledge a little covert Duck who lends me the courage to share my imagination on the page, and not quit... even when other people don't hear the little quacker.

Diana Kathryn

Table of Contents

Chasing the Enemy

It must have been kismet, or fate, or something, but when I got up that morning, I was startled to find that my pet parakeet, Destiny, had escaped from her cage. I don't remember forgetting to click the latch closed the night before, after feeding her... but I can't really be sure, I was pretty hammered. It had been a long day at the office, and I allowed myself a little social sedative therapy to help me forget. A friend called just as I was leaving the office, asked me out for drinks, and – long story short – the bird was now gone, and I was enduring a serious headache, the likes of which haven't been experienced since my failed attempt at running with the bulls. But that's another story.

I looked everywhere for the ridiculous little bird, following tiny tufts of blue down feathers around my living room. It's not that I particularly liked the bird. She was a gift from my younger brother, a one-time wannabe bird breeder. He promised me, when he'd decided to get out of the bird breeding business to become a suspension bridge salesman, and she was his last hatchling, that parakeets were gentle, fragile creatures. He promised me that she would die before the end of the month. "After all," he said, "she's already nearly a year old. How long can a parakeet possibly last?" he asked in his rhetorical 'don't you dare try to answer that question' tone. So I took the bird. Two years later, and she was still hanging on, squawking for her breakfast every morning like some demon from the ashes of a charred castle during the height of the Crusades.

Destiny had deserted me, and although I was secretly elated at the prospect of the silent meditation such an event would bring into my life, I'm also an animal lover, which means it was imperative that I find her and make sure she wasn't injured. If she had found another human – or perhaps a parakeet family to spend her time with – I would give her my blessing, of course. But until I knew her fate, for sure, I couldn't let go of Destiny.

Not finding a trace of her in the apartment but noticing that I'd left the window over the kitchen sink ajar, I ventured onto the snowy streets in search of her. I wasn't convinced that a parakeet could survive in Michigan's first real snow of the year... three inches of stupid white... she's a small bird, and I knew I wouldn't be able to sleep until I knew that I'd done all I could to bring Destiny back to me... or at least witness her untimely demise and thereby absolve myself of further guilt.

Out of some sort of strange, distorted desperation, I began singing a hung-over version of "Grandma Got Run Over By A Reindeer," thinking that a song might appeal to her... while secretly hoping it wouldn't. Birds really don't make great pets; well, at least not parakeets. They're noisy, make a terrible mess in the bottom of the cage, and aren't really all that snuggly. I'm more of a dog person, myself. But, once you take in an animal, just like little brothers, they become a part of your family – whether you truly enjoy having them around or not. Without Destiny, my life would be lacking something... intangible. It was important that I did all I could do to find her.

I'd walked about seven blocks, then turned on my heels for the frigid walk back home, when I spied her perched on the low branch of a nearby tree. She was easy to spot... blue fluff on a three-inch line of pure white. When she saw me, she immediately began singing a beautiful rendition of some classic hymn, I think... though I'm not sure where she ever would have heard it; I'm a country music fan, myself. As I stood watching her, gently coaxing her down to me (for truly, she was a part of my family), a bystander of indiscriminate origin sidled up to me and said, "Whatcha doin' there?"

"I have to get her to come to me," I replied, keeping my eyes on the bird.

"Why?" asked the bystander. "What's so special 'bout such a little bird?"

"It's Destiny. I invited her in, and life would be lost to me without her."

"Huh," said the bystander, looking first to me and then up to the bird with unabashed confusion.

Destiny, upon hearing my declaration, sincere in its tenor, flew down to my left shoulder, where she sat, contented in her life's validation.

"Well, what'da know..." said the bystander. "It looks like Destiny has got your back."

The bystander walked away as I felt the sickening warmth of bird poop seep into my sweater.

A Sore Loser

She was everything her mother told her not to be, and still, it hadn't made a difference. Raised in a highly conservative family with the tumult of propriety everywhere she turned, it was difficult to win. She dressed well, had impeccable manners, and a dowry large enough to capture preeminent suitors... and still, it wasn't enough. She wanted something more, something different.

One day, he came to her door, roses in one hand, and a proposal of marriage in the other. Of course, her parents approved; he was from good stock and had a bank balance that mirrored his social standing. He was the finest champagne of men, bubbling refinement and promising a life of forever bliss. In her soul, she knew it was a scam, but went along anyway; accepting the loss of any individuality she may have attained had she played the game differently.

Three years later, they had two delightful children, and a nanny to care for them. She pranced the social scene unencumbered by poverty or guilt, making good use of charity to fill her lost evenings. He immersed himself in his work and was rarely present – physically, emotionally, spiritually, sexually, or in nearly every other way – except financially. It's what kept her content. And still, it wasn't enough. She wanted something more, something different. She'd lost the teenage fantasy of her white knight; and she accepted that loss with the daily immersion of false prophets who regaled her with the hint of emancipation through prayer, wine, and tolerance. The effect was only slightly comforting.

Twenty years passed. The children were grown and moved on to take up residence in the finest Universities in Europe, chasing dreams and catching rainbows. They weren't yet satisfied – but they were working at it, fervently. She envied their opportunity and courage. She'd lost all of that with the acceptance of a rose on the veranda of a summer afternoon.

She remained at home, fighting off the jealousies of women who floated ghost-like through her marriage; never truly discovering *her* path of least resistance. Agitation and quiet rage, she came to understand, could not compete with the undulation of apathy or the small flame of happiness she dared to reach for; the singe of its heat eluding her. She wanted nothing more. She'd lost the spark.

When he died tragically, on a ferry while commuting home from his latest lover's chateau, of a brain aneurysm, she did not weep for him. Why should she? She'd lost the continuance she'd been dependent on for thirty years, and she was irritated that he'd left her the burden of their vast estate. There were lawyers to handle the delicate complications, of course; but she was saddled with the annoyances of the daily ills of maintenance. She'd lost the recumbent lifestyle to which she had become accustomed. She was on her feet now, more than was comfortable; a telephone relentlessly dangling within reach as she was forced to make decisions, choose paths that could never relinquish resistance, and parent her grown children a continent away.

She resented all he had left her. She resented all he had done to keep her placid throughout the decades they'd been together. She resented the plans she was now forced to make in order to preserve the children's entitlement program. She'd never wanted any of this. Now that she'd lost the key to her self-loathing with no target of amiable anxiety, she resented herself.

The housekeeper found her a month after his death, her naked body draped with the jewels of his false remorse; her head lying on a pillow of the pages of his portfolio, stained with the blood of her awareness. She'd left the world lost in a sea of heaving self-doubt. She'd had it all, she'd lost nothing tangible, only the love she never possessed; and yet, she rallied against her privilege and resented the moment he'd left her with responsibility.

She hadn't coped with losing well.

Grumpy's Testimony

From the Desk of Max Ink, Daily News Court Reporter; June 14: Far Away Enchanted Kingdom Circuit Court Part Three

The bailiff takes his place at the front of the room and brings the gallery to order. "All rise. Court is now in session. The honorable Judge Fairness, presiding."

The judge bangs his gavel. "Take your seats, please." He acknowledges the defendant and the plaintiff sitting at their respective tables, and nods to their attorneys. He looks to the defense attorney, "Call your first witness."

"Mr. Snide, counsel for the defense, Queen Anais, your honor. On this third day of due process, we call Mr. Grumpy Dwarf to the stand."

Mr. Grumpy Dwarf shuffles up to the witness box, his hat in his hand, and a scowl on his face.

Mr. Snide sidles up to the witness box, the pants of his perfectly tailored suit holding their creases flawlessly as he walked. "Now, Mr. Dwarf..." begins Mr. Snide.

"The name's Grumpy, if ya don't mind," he says with a grumble and a sneer.

"Yes, certainly. Grumpy; as you've already been sworn in, please tell the court, in your own words, what transpired during the week in question."

"Trainspired?" says Grumpy.

"Yes," says Snide. "What *happened*?"

"Ah... you gots some fancy words, don'tcha, mister? Well, I suppose it started off as any other regular week. Me an' the boys were headin' off to the mines to dig for stuff like we always do. And when we come back, this... this hussy was in our house! Downright rude, if ya ask me."

"Is the woman you speak of in in the courtroom today?" asks Snide.

"Yes, sir. She's sitting right there." Grumpy points his stubby left thumb at Snow White, sitting at the plaintiff's table. He points with his thumb, because he lost the first two fingers of that hand some years ago in a mining accident. It's only part of the reason for his sullied mood; but that's another story.

"If it pleases the court, let the record reflect that Grumpy Dwarf has indicated Ms. Snow White. Go on, Grumpy. Continue with your account."

"I ain't givin' ya no money, mister!" roils Grumpy.

"No, sir, not money... your account... your story of what happened that week," corrects Mr. Snide. He waggles his head in disbelief and not quite loud enough for the jury to hear chides, "Where did they find this guy? He's a moron!"

"Well, like I said, we was headin' back from the mines, all hungry an' such, jus' looking for a little dinner an' rest, when that... that... argh!" Grumpy's face turns bright crimson and his beard prickles away from his face, making him look like a startled porcupine.

"Calm down Grumpy, sir. Just tell us what transpired," reminds Mr. Snide.

"Fine," he says, clearing the anger from his throat. "She comes into our house, uninvited an' starts rummagin' around. She moved stuff we didn't want moved... ya know, cobwebs an' such. She washed the dishes that we'd on purpose left in the sink... no need for her to do that, we gots more. An' she MADE THE BEDS, TOO! The gall, I tell ya! An' then, when we got home, she made us BATHE! I don't know who this harlot thought she was, struttin' into our home as if she ran the place. The others... well... they went right along... swayed by a pretty face, they were. But not me. Oh no! I stood my ground. I told 'em, we can't keep her. She's not a puppy, after all. An' for my mind, a heap more trouble! I knew somebody would be missing her an' come for her... an' wreck our lives even more than this one already done did. I reckon'd they'd even come for the mine. But did the boys listen to me... NO! They just pranced around the house like Dopey, there... all twitter-pated with stupidity. It was disgraceful."

"Then what happened, Mr. Grumpy?" cajoled Mr. Snide once again.

"Well, it was just as I told 'em... but they didn't want to listen to me, NO! Those ingrates... sometimes I think the lot of 'em is just simply daft. Stark crazy, I tell ya!" Grumpy was working himself up into a genuine froth now... spittle dripping from the corner of his mouth where he lost some control in that past mining accident... but I digress.

Mr. Snide enjoyed the theatrics of his star witness and egged him on further. "Go on, sir... just recount the facts for the court. How did things change for your clan after Snow White entered your lives?"

"Well, as I said, the day of reckonin' finally came. She didn't listen to us... let some stranger into the house... and BAM! Next thing we know, she's layin' on the floor, near dead. I said good riddance to ya... but the boys... those foolish curs, they were smitten. Brainwashed, I tell ya! They actually wanted to put her in some stupid glass box to keep her forever. We're miners, for crimaney's sake, not taxidermists! I jus' don't know what they were thinkin'. The whole thing was like making gold out of a box of rocks, I tell ya!"

"Please continue..." Snide encouraged, eager to capture his audience with the climax of the story.

"Well, that's when it happened," said Grumpy in a voice that was almost a whisper – quite the feat for such a crotchety old man.

Mr. Snide leaned in real close, his voice low and his body tense. "What, Mr. Grumpy, what happened?"

"We had to deal with... with... I can hardly say it..." Grumpy looked away from Snide, toward the townsfolk in the jury box. His face held the shame he knew was real.

"Go ahead," said Mr. Snide. "Take your time... find your words, Mr. Grumpy. What did you have to deal with?" Snide was waiting for the magnificent punchline he knew would sway this case.

"LOVE!" howled Grumpy.

Mr. Snide took a step back, eyed the jury with a heavily loaded pregnant pause, and said, "Love, sir?"

"Yes, LOVE!" bellowed Grumpy. "It's outrageous! We'd never had to deal with that infernal nonsense before. Our lives were simple... we went to the mine every day, did our work, came home, ate a bit, slept a bit, an' got up the next day to do it all again. We had a good life! An' then, this... this... wretched female come along an' made us all care for her! She wrecked everything! Bollixed up the whole works, I tell ya! Now, we had this woman to care for... an' she took her toll on us, I might tell ya! All that washin', an' proper table manners, an' makin' the beds each morning... It was ridiculous. We had a good life before she came... an' then she went and complicated it all to pieces! The nerve of that woman! The boys an' I actually started CARING. ARGH! It's enough to drive a person daft, I tell ya!"

Grumpy took a moment to look around the room for some sign that he'd made his point... knowing that surely, there would be others in the courtroom who heard his plight and understood. Blank faces stared back at him. Grumpy went on with his story, hopeful that someone would understand and be on his side.

"An' then, when she was lying there, in that pretty box, sleeping an' such... well, I thought that finally we were rid of her. Finally, we could have our lives back. No more washin'... no more cleanin'... and no more CARING. But she couldn't leave well enough alone... No! Not this one. No sir!" He thrust his stubby thumb at Snow White again, punctuating his disdain.

Mr. Snide coaxed him again, directing the play with just as much intensity as he thought the judge would allow. "We want to hear your story, Mr. Grumpy. Tell us what happened."

"Well, this fancy pants prince come along and kissed her! Can ya imagine... the unmitigated nerve of the fellow... I mean KISSING a near-dead lady. Have ya ever heard such nonsense!" Grumpy spat his disgust at the prince who sat beside Snow White.

"What happened after the kiss, Mr. Grumpy?" cajoled Snide, again.

"Well, she surprised us all, she did. She sat right up an' kissed him right back. Then she jumped out of her glass box, an' said that we were all going to live with this Mr. Fancy Pants at his castle someplace farther away from the mine. What right did she have to say where we would live? An' we didn't have no say in it, neither. It's just wrong, I tell ya!" Grumpy's face again lit up like Rudolph's red nose, his whiskers alive with static electricity.

"So," interjected Mr. Snide, "she wanted to essentially kidnap you, and take you away from the only home you've ever known? Is that right, sir?" Snide had a cat-ate-the-canary grin on his face. He was proud of his star witness. "Grumpy sure is hitting this one out of the park," he murmured to no one in particular.

"Darn right, that's right! An' she ain't got no right! I'm still the only one in charge of me... Ain't nothin' gonna change that." Grumpy pounded his fist on the witness box and looked adamantly at the judge. "It's criminal, I tell ya! Just criminal! She should be in jail or somethin'. It just ain't right!" The judge sat stoic... unaffected by the theatrics.

"Thank you, Mr. Grumpy." said Mr. Snide. "You may step down."

The judge banged his gavel on the desk once again. "Okay folks. We'll take a short recess and return for Mr. Sneezy's testimony after lunch. Court is adjourned."

Anger and Grief: Two Sides of The Same Coin

"Anger suffers as grief withdraws." At least that's what my shrink told me as I clutched the pillow to my chest, watching the heartless snow fall upon his Cambridge window pane. He said, "Don't worry Amy, as your grief goes away, so will your anger; for the two cannot live without each other. They feed on each other. Grief soothes anger. Anger feeds grief. When you can bring yourself to let go of one, the other will also disappear. It's the simple nature of things."

As I wrote the check and dropped it in the competent hands of his secretary, I left that session with a new appreciation for life, death, anger, grief, and the stupidity of psychoanalysis.

Simply put, my Harvard educated, psychobabble wielding, one-hundred-dollar-per-hour egomaniac analyst was wrong. Good old doctor What's It got it wrong. After the few brief months of the all-consuming grief of my mother's passing subsided, the anger remained... and in full force; albeit just under the surface of my daily life; irritating every thought, every decision, every joy.

Each day, I recalled the fact that my mother, with whom I had parted company on less-than-stellar terms, was no longer in my life. And I was still angry about the fact. I was angry that our last conversation together was not a pleasant one; and angry that she had refused to do anything to improve her situation in life... for years.

As I walked the snow-covered streets from the T-station back to my apartment on Boylston Street, I rehashed the frustration, reinvigorating the anger with each sloshing step of boot against icy pavement. My mother had spent the last five years self-medicating and ignoring the advice of doctors; claiming, "They don't really know what they're talking about and clearly, I know my body much better than they do. After all, I live with it every day."

Our heated phone call ended with my telling her, "After four years of medical school, four years of residency, and who knows how many years in practice affiliated with a top-rated hospital, you're going to question your cardiologist?"

She said, "I don't want to discuss this anymore." And there was silence on the line. She had hung up on her daughter. The whole thing was nuts! And so, without much fanfare, she died three weeks later. She had a heart attack on Easter morning. I didn't expect her resurrection, even though she had been baptized not many years before in the very same waters where John had dunked Jesus.

As the grief withdrew, the anger swelled within me, tainting my memory of her and the childhood we shared. The anger that lingered made me question the happy memories I had of her... made me question my relationship with her... made me question – albeit briefly – my actions as a mother. I had vowed not to follow in her negative footsteps, and only resole the positive steps. Would I do that? The anger of her passing made me question far too much. And the grief no longer consoled.

When I brought this inconsistency to the attention of dear Dr. What's It, all he could say was, "Everyone grieves differently, Amy. Your process is unlike anyone else's."

Then why, I thought, *am I paying you ridiculous amounts of money each month to convince me there are rules to these things, and answers easily found if I sacrifice my most conflicting thoughts on your couch of absolution?*

That was the last time Dr. What's It and I spent any time together. I don't miss him, and I doubt he misses me.

It's been over a year now, and I've made peace with my anger... dislodged my grief... and subsisted on the understanding that we all do the work we must in this world, to get by.

And for those of us who don't, well, we get what we get. We, sooner or later, become comfortable with our discomfort when reflecting on the aftermath, and the weekly payments that support the many Dr. What's It's kids through college.

Conspiracy Theorists Convention

It was the usual crowd you'd see at these sorts of events; rack selections from Old Navy, Macey's, L.L. Bean, and a few custom jobs from Rodeo Drive. Stereotypes were frequently assumed, few lived outside of what their costumes described. Occasionally, you'd find one or two who managed a bit of authentic sheen, but it was rare. As they milled about, over-imbibing and over-exaggerating, popular lyrics could be recognized by anyone who'd attended in years past.

"When the wife and me were on vacation in the desert of Peru," one man began, draping his very drunken arm around a nearby companion, "we visited the Nazca Lines, you know, those famous crop circle things, and everything looked like it did in that Discovery Channel documentary, except one thing. There was a porcupine carved in the ground. Can you believe it! A blasted porcupine right there in the dirt!" He slapped his companion on the back, nearly toppling himself to the ground, yet salvaging each and every one of his Scotch-drenched ice cubes. "We saw it from the helicopter. Now, I ask you, how is that possible? I don't even think they *have* porcupines in Peru. It's got to be aliens, right?! What else could do that? Eons of fast-moving water during the time of the dinosaurs, or even all the years after, couldn't possibly be that precise or that creative. We're being lied to, make no mistake. There's something much bigger going on here!"

"The same thing happened at Roswell, am I right?" chimed in another zealot. "I know there has to be a bigger story there. Weather balloons and fake alien autopsies, come on! How does anyone believe that nonsense? I'm ex-military," he said with a left-handed salute that nearly cold-cocked a passerby, "and I tell you, there's simply no reason to have a military base in the middle of the dessert and claim it doesn't exist. The point of *having* a base is to intimidate the other guys. And once they're discovered, why would they claim that it's for 'secret' testing of aircraft and other military stuff? I'm telling you straight," he said with an air of superiority, "if you wanted a base to be secret, you'd put it inside of a mountain or twenty thousand leagues under the sea, not right out in the open where people driving by and satellites can find it. I was a pilot," he said, pulling at the left lapel of his sport coat where a small gold airplane pin sat perched, "it *must* be a tarmac for incoming aliens. Why else would they deny its existence?"

"You're right," said a woman who had been eavesdropping from inside her less-than-interesting hen clutch. "No one would believe that... but the bigger question is, why do they keep propagating these lies? What are they trying to distract us from... what heinous, horrific thing is happening right under our noses that they don't want us to discover? It's like world-wide magician's slight-of-hand." The men nodded in agreement. "It's like they're trying to confuse us with the strange, flashy thing right in front of us to avoid drawing attention to the fact that they're pulling the wires off stage." The men raised their glasses in a toast, and the group clinked in unison, adding their stamp of approval to her proclamation.

As the assembly gradually moved from standing to taking chairs at banquet tables scattered about the hall, their attention was quickly drawn to the small stage at the front of the room. One of the event organizers tapped the microphone at the podium and began his speech, continuing the common conversations from the collection of believers without segue or introduction. "It's our fundamental right as human beings to know the truth about our own origins."

Applause swelled. Some members tapped knives to glasses in support of the speaker's remarks.

"Government agencies, in partnership with religious organizations, have been keeping us deluded for far too long. They tell us that the carvings we see in crop circles and the indentations at Nazca are simply geological malformations, and that we are manipulating our own vision to feed some psychological desire to describe something we can't or don't want to understand."

Boos and hisses radiated from the floor with a rhythmic chanting of "Lies, it's all lies!" Once the commotion began to subside, the speaker continued.

"They tell us there's a rational explanation. They filibuster our intellect from the time we're in grade school until we are middle-aged adults, when finally, we believe their storylines without question. 'It's a hoax;' they claim."

More hisses, jeers, and sneers came from the crowd.

"'It's a naturally occurring phenomenon;' they say."

"No way!" yelled a group of twenty-somethings to the right.

"Yet we understand the truth. We *have* been visited, and we *will be* visited again... and the time is growing very near!"

Applause bounced off the ceiling tiles and spilled out into the foyer from the hotel's grand ballroom.

"Scour away all the nonsense and allow the truth to be seen in its full glory, this should be our rallying cry," the speaker hollered as he pounded his fist on the podium. "The government can't keep us from knowing, especially if what they withhold could affect our safety."

"We want the Truth!" screamed a pack of millennials to the right.

"We are entitled to protect ourselves and our families. If we *have* been visited by aliens, and those of us here tonight are certain that we have, how do we know that these extraterrestrials haven't made a deal with Washington to annihilate us all when the time is right? Make no mistake, such a treaty would be easily cast if it meant bank accounts would be swollen and interstellar cushions would soften their descent when there are no other options left. Let's face it, our government is not now, and never has been, operating in our best interests. The alien coverup is just a small piece of that pie."

More applause and cheers erupted from the audience as waiters and waitresses worked hard to refill water glasses without becoming drenched by overturned tableware.

"In spite of this, now is the time that we must play possum, draw back, and allow the insolents to falter with their counterfeit compass. They will stumble as they saunter toward the door of what they believe to be an easy exit. Only then will they fall victim to the same slight-of-hand that they have been perpetrating against us all these decades." The woman at table eight nodded and offered her new friends a smug grin.

"Once we pull back, relent, stop pressing for answers; only then will they make the mistake that will divulge their true intentions, and *they will be betrayed*. That's when we'll catch them in their deception and set in motion our mutiny, thrashing hard at their political solar plexus, and forcing out the flatulence of their duplicity."

The crowd exploded with cheers of "mutiny" and "hit 'em where it hurts", accompanied by clinking stemware, high-fives, and gregarious pats on the back. This amalgamation of different thinkers trusted strongly in their own rhetoric and weren't going to be persuaded otherwise.

As the rabble continued congratulating themselves and began comparing notes about their most excellent plan, a stout little man with rounded posture approached the dais. He wore tan khakis and the brown cardigan of honorable respect, as would a veteran of the Normandy invasion. Still, his head held no hair nor hat, his dark eyes were shaped like almonds, his tiny nose appeared to be lacking cartilage, and his ears were flat to the side of his head. His skin held a grey pallor that gave the impression of a foreboding illness. The crowd was drawn to their feet as they felt the energy of his approach. None could explain their silence nor their fragility in his presence. There was an electric charge to the air.

He stepped up to the podium and adjusted the microphone. "I've been sent to give you a message," he intoned with the gentle expression of somebody's great-grandfather. He reached for a bottle of water from the nearby table, and as he took a long draw, a voice could be heard from the back of the crowd. A middle-aged woman stepped from the camouflage of the throng and shouted the words many were thinking.

"I know the truth... you can't hide from me," she said, thrusting her arm forward and pointing directly at the little man. "You're a GREY! Don't deny it... you're an alien sent to give us the final ultimatum!"

"No," he said calmly, putting the water bottle aside, unbuttoning his sweater, and allowing it to fall to the floor. "My name is Michael," he roared as bright white wings unfolded from the hunch on his back, "and God is very displeased!"

Fire and Water

The day began as most other days did. Coffee, bacon, toast with strawberry jam. Brian enjoyed the solitude of morning more than any other time of day. It was quiet, calm, and filled with possibilities. Today was Thursday, one more day and the week would be over, and he could relax through the weekend. His plan was to escape to the lake, a fishing trip was just what his soul needed to recharge from all the frustration of this latest job. He was well paid for his trouble, but nothing could compensate him for the headaches. He'd had enough.

A carpenter for nearly fourteen years, and foreman on this job, he'd never encountered as many problems building a house. The mansion in the hills had seven bathrooms, and it still wasn't enough to process all the excrement he'd had to manage over the past two years. The owner and architect changed the building plans so many times that it was making Brian's head swim. "Move that wall five feet to the east, but don't lose the wonderful line of sight through the gigantic window in the next room." And, "I'd really like paving stones for the sidewalk instead of concrete, they look so much nicer. Can we do paving stones, in blush?"

Or, her latest request, "I know we've already finished the master bath, but can we add a fireplace near the tub? It'll make the room so much cozier."

The Diva that owned the place had a penchant for causing trouble, and it followed her everywhere. Brian complained to the architect, but it did him little good. She was adamant, claiming cost was not an issue… and then whined when he told her the budget had to be reworked to accommodate her laundry list of changes. This final change, the gold-plated fireplace in the master bathroom, would be the final change. After this, the house would be done, and he would be, too.

It was one o'clock in the afternoon when he got the call. Brian's mother had been rushed to the hospital from her nursing home in the throes of severe renal failure. Evidently, even after twelve years of dialysis, Martha's left kidney still didn't understand the role it played in keeping her alive. Brian called the Diva to explain the situation and let her know that the fireplace would be installed first thing in the morning. She wailed inconsolably about being abandoned and tried to ply him with more money to have it finished that night. Brian apologized and hung up the phone, not allowing her to delay his escape. He needed to be by his mother's side. Her life meant more to him than any six-figure income an empty-brained manicure could ever offer, even if she was married to a Congressman.

When Brian arrived at the hospital, he was quietly ushered into his mother's room by the attending nurse. The nurse explained that not only was Martha's left kidney shutting down (she'd lost the right one years ago), but to add insult to injury, her diabetes had been affected by a whacked-out sugar level, a complication of the problem in processing insulin. This detail was nothing new, her sugar had a habit of spiking frequently, but it did make matters worse, and now her heart and blood pressure were in agony. Martha's face was pale, and her eyelids fluttered as she worked in vain to maintain consciousness. She was next on the transplant list, but chances were slim she would get it in time.

Brian kissed his mother on the forehead, squeezed her cold, clammy hand, and left the room, unable to stomach the frustration of being so helpless in her presence, even with all his money. He walked to the parking lot and lit a cigarette. Not sure what he could do to help, but feeling he had to do something, he stewed in anger and guilt.

After ten minutes of pacing, he pulled out his cell phone and made the call he had been avoiding.

"It's me. Yeah, things are at rock bottom. I think we need to do the thing."

"Are you sure?" asked Sam.

"Yes. It's time." Brian's stomach lurched, nearly voiding his breakfast.

"Okay, if you say so. It's the standard agreement, fifty now, and another two hundred when the job is done. I'll send the address for the drop," he said.

"Got it. How soon will we have an answer?"

"By supper tonight. That do it for you?"

"It's cutting it close, but it'll have to do."

Brian hung up the phone and waited for the text message with an address to appear. He lit another cigarette and paced the full length of the parking lot twice before his phone chimed with the text. He got in his car and drove to the bank. The long line made him uncomfortable, but he forced himself to stay calm. In his business, withdrawing large sums of cash wasn't usually an issue. Gold-plated vanity sinks, pewter clawfoot tubs, fifteen-foot-tall stained-glass bay windows... it all added up. The transaction took less than five minutes. He was a very good customer.

Brian dropped the green duffle at the location he'd been given and drove back to the hospital to be with Martha for one more hour... one last day... before...

Martha passed gently in her sleep that night, with Brian holding her hand and singing softly. *"Amazing Grace"* was a favorite old hymn, and she especially loved it when sung to the tune of "*The House of The Rising Sun*". Martha was a walking dichotomy in so many areas of her life, a trait she'd always hoped her son would inherit. "Always live life walking upon the path of what is least expected," she'd told him. "Always keep them guessing."

The next morning, he spent an hour on the phone, planning the details for Martha's cremation. There would be no service, she wanted an anonymous exit. The gentleman at the funeral home ended their conversation with, "Not to worry. We'll handle everything, sir." Brian returned to the house in the hills for one last walk-through and to install that blasted fireplace.

Friday evening, the news could not be ignored.

"The new home of Congressman Michael Fieldstone and his wife, Shelly, was incinerated in an apparent gas leak blast. The Fieldstones were not hurt, as they had not yet moved into the house. There was one tragic casualty, however. Thirty-seven-year-old Brian Botox, the construction foreman who was putting the finishing touches on the home, installing a gold-trimmed, gas fireplace in the master bathroom. Botox's friends and colleagues are claiming foul-play and calling for a full investigation. They insist that this accident was not an accident, but murder. His associates claim that the gas line was in proper working order, that Brian

Botox had fourteen years in the industry, and would never be so careless as to forget to turn off the gas line before installing a fireplace.

"The authorities, however, are convinced it was simply a tragic accident, nothing more. Congressman Fieldstone, in response to the overwhelming community pressure, has instructed police to open a case file and look into the matter, leaving no stone unturned. Human remains were discovered in the ashes of the house. The investigators are assuming they are those of Brian Botox, as he is unaccounted for at this time. Heartbreakingly, Mr. Botox just lost his mother Thursday night from complications due to renal failure. He had no other family. After the investigation concludes, and a thorough clean-up of the debris, the Fieldstones plan to put the property up for sale."

****

"It's a live one!" squealed Brian, sounding like a six-year-old boy, as he reeled in the line.

"Yup," Sam hollered from the boat's fly deck as he tossed back his Scotch. "The Mediterranean sure is nice this time of year."

The Strange and Obscure Clearing House Sweepstakes Giveaway Contest

Congratulations! You have been specially selected to participate in *The Strange And Obscure Clearing House Sweepstakes Giveaway Contest!*

It's not every day that an opportunity as rare as this lands in your mailbox... be impressed!

The rules are simple ... the prizes Strange and Obscure ... the opportunity for fame and fortune nearly non-existent ... but that's not why we do these things, is it?! No! We do these things because Obscure Strangeness found in the everyday should be revered, celebrated, and obsessed over. After all, cubicle life isn't all it's cracked up to be, now is it!?

So yes, you have been selected to engage in the beside-the-norm-silliness of *The Strange And Obscure Clearing House Sweepstakes Giveaway Contest*. Rejoice appropriately.

Now, you might be asking yourself, "Self, why should I do this thing?" Well, if yourself is intrigued by the oddity of the letter now sitting on your kitchen counter or laying gently in your hands, yourself might say, "Well, clearly, someone has gone to extensive lengths to add a little nuttiness to my day, and I should play along, if for no other reason than to see where it all ends up."

Or, if yourself is of the trusting nature and is undaunted by the Strangeness of the paperwork now spread out all over the dining room table, yourself might say, "What harm could it really do; I mean, really, could something Strange And Obscure be all that dangerous?"

Or, if yourself is of the paranoid nature, yourself might say something like, "Well, I'd better see this thing through to the end because it might come back to bite me in the butt if I don't. After all, you never know how vindictive even your silliest friends can get."

Or, if yourself is the analytical type who understands that you simply have "interesting," easily emotionally wounded friends, yourself might say, "Okay, what the hell, I'll play along. After all, if I don't, I could scar the emotional psyche of my friend for life, convincing them that they have no one who really understands them; and they may think that I don't truly like them, because I won't play this silly game with them, and that might cause irreparable damage that will stand the test of time and probably haunt their soul forever, never allowing them the peace and comfort death might have otherwise brought in their final moments."

So, you'll play along? Fantastic!

This is a contest with simple rules, and easy to follow directions…

Rule #1: You must complete the enclosed *Strange And Obscure Clearing House Sweepstakes Giveaway Contest* Entry Form in its entirety. Missing answers will disqualify your *Strange And Obscure Clearing House Sweepstakes Giveaway Contest* Entry Form and you will forfeit any and all opportunities to win any and all of *The Strange And Obscure Clearing House Sweepstakes Giveaway Contest* Prizes.

Rule #2: You must return the enclosed *Strange And Obscure Clearing House Sweepstakes Giveaway Contest* Entry Form by the official *Strange And Obscure Clearing House Sweepstakes Giveaway Contest* Entry Deadline. Late entries will cause you to forfeit any and all opportunities to win any and all of *The Strange And Obscure Clearing House Sweepstakes Giveaway Contest* Prizes. And, you'd be blowing a chance to see how it all ends, and where's the fun in that?

Rule #3: You must complete all the answers on the enclosed *Strange And Obscure Clearing House Sweepstakes Giveaway Contest* Entry Form in **<u>Purple</u>** pencil, ink, or crayon. Why? Because it's Strange And Obscure, that's why! If you haven't figured that part out yet, you will most certainly need help completing *The Strange And Obscure Clearing House Sweepstakes Giveaway Contest* Entry Form! Get help from someone you trust, not just some fly-by-night attorney who enjoys a good laugh.

Rule #4: *The Strange And Obscure Clearing House Sweepstakes Giveaway Contest* Entry Deadline is 168 hours from the time you open the envelope. Of course, there will be clandestine shadow-walkers watching your every move, and watching the clock... you won't see them, but they will see you (undress with the shades drawn, they're kind of Strange in an Obscure sort of way). If your *Strange And Obscure Clearing House Sweepstakes Giveaway Contest* Entry Form is even one moment late in reaching your local postal repository, you will be disqualified. Don't test us on this point... we mean business!

Now, if you are an over-achiever, eager-beaver and have completed your *Strange And Obscure Clearing House Sweepstakes Giveaway Contest* Entry Form early and would like to return your *Strange And Obscure Clearing House Sweepstakes Giveaway Contest* Entry Form early, you may do so... at your own risk, of course. Remember, life is full of risk... and that's why this game is so very enjoyable, you never can tell, can you!

And that's it. Pretty easy. Four simply stated, easy to read rules without ambiguity or confusion. Don't you just love it when a plan comes together!

So, now you're thinking to yourself, "Self, what kinds of Strange And Obscure Prizes could I win?" And we're so glad yourself was inquisitive enough to ask such a great question... Tell them what they might win, Bob!

Well Ted, first up is the **Snazzy Snowman Family Kit**. Your snowman family will be dressed to the nines and ready to horrify the neighborhood the way all good snow sentries should! This forty-seven-piece snow metamorphosis kit includes felt a fedora for Snow Dad to give him that respectable look, and a baseball cap for Snow Son to convey that timeless innocence. Also included are matching "Santa" hats for Snow Mother and Snow Daughter because we all know that when mothers and daughters dress alike, they appear less sinister. Scarves for the entire Snow Family will keep out winter's chill while they are busy spying on your unsuspecting neighbors. Plastic carrot noses as well as pieces of coal to make up the eyes and mouths keep things "real" and a wood pipe helps Snow Dad look less menacing.

We've also included super snazzy buttons to keep up the illusion that your snow family is dressed, and really isn't as depraved as some might think – you never know when the Neighborhood Watch is on patrol! Everything stores from year-to-year in a personalized, hand-painted 12 ¾" x 7¼" x 5¾" wood chest with brass hinges and a stainless-steel latch so you can continue to torture your neighbors with Strange And Obscure Snow Stalkers year after year. Surely, a Strange And Obscure Prize every contestant will be clamoring for!

Our next Strange And Obscure Prize is an **Udderly Irresistible Cow Wall Clock**! This unique, one of a kind (not really, I think they made several thousand) kitchen clock comes complete with a bread pan face and serving spoon ears. This fabulous clock is handmade from recycled kitchen pieces to form a cow with character. Set this cheerful wall clock in your kitchen and you'll start every day off with a smile and a moo; and she'll make sure you're not late for work, too. This Obscure cow hangs on your kitchen wall and only uses up 9¼" x 8¾" of space. Surely, every milk-loving, cheese-loving, steak-loving family will cherish this clock for generations. It will become a valued family heirloom, for sure! No harm has befallen knives and forks in the fabricating of this clock.

Our final Strange And Obscure Prize is **A MASSIVE SECRET**. Ooooh, I can hear the gasps of exhilaration flowing through the crowd. This Strange And Obscure Prize grows with intensity and excitement the more we talk about it.

If you are fortunate enough to win this Obscure prize, you will hear a knocking at your door one Strange and Obscure night to be greeted by one of our Obscurely Strange shadow-walkers. Do not be alarmed, they mean you no harm. They are your guides into an evening of Obscurity and Strangeness unlike any other you will ever experience. They will blindfold you and whisk you away to a Strange And

Obscure "abandoned warehouse" in an unspecified location. There, you will endure moments of building tension as you try, without fail, to discern where you have been taken. Without physical torture (although some tickling may be involved) we will give you clues to help you determine your location and the course of events to be experienced throughout the night.

It's all a **GINORMOUS SECRET**, so we can't tell you much, but we can tell you that your evening will be filled with Strangeness, Obscurity, and memories to last a lifetime! Unfortunately, because the "abandoned warehouse" is in an unspecified location we can't give you an emergency number for relatives to find you; bring your cell phone.

Welcome To The World Of *The Strange And Obscure Clearing House Sweepstakes Giveaway Contest* and Good Luck!

Your Strange and Obscure Clearing House Sweepstakes Contest entry deadline starts **NOW**!

Reunion Redux

The room was filled with the biggest throwback collection he'd ever seen. Jason coerced him into attending the reunion and he wasn't happy he'd allowed himself to be talked into it. He'd caved, for reasons surpassing understanding, and he now stood surrounded by a multitude he couldn't remember, most of whom he never really liked in the first place. Although the Facebook event page made it clear the dress code was mandatory, he refused to do the costume thing... dressing in that style turned his stomach when it was in fashion thirty-five years ago, he certainly wasn't going to do it tonight.

Seeing the look of horror on his face when they walked in the room, Jason said, "Come on, it won't be that bad. Let's get a drink, it'll settle your nerves."

"Yeah, I don't think that's possible... but I guess it couldn't hurt," Matthew said, shuffling after his friend and working hard at remaining as inconspicuous as possible.

Over the next hour or so, a parade of people, some who were familiar and others whose faces Matthew couldn't completely place, sidled up to the two of them at the bar. Refrains of "Hey, we were in drafting together;" or "I remember you, best place-kicker we ever had;" and his favorite, "I think we had

Algebra together, but I only saw you in class once", competed with the squealing, hugging mob of women near the door. Then came the expected parade of guys from the team, each one slapping his back with that superficial locker room bravado he'd always detested. Matthew passed each visitor off to another unknown verbal assailant as quickly as possible and moved to the far end of the hall. He hid near the stage where the band was performing a poor imitation of what was once good music.

That's when he saw her... three o'clock, twenty feet, and closing in fast. He could have found her in the room blindfolded. She was preceded by the same perfume, and even all these years later, the wiggle in her walk that drove so many to drink or worse... himself included... was as captivating as ever. His heart raced as she drew near, and he secretly wished himself invisible.

"Wow! Amanda, it's been a long time. How've you been?" he stammered above the din of the music. He took a sip of his drink for courage as he waited for her reply.

"Good, Matthew, I got married, and we have a son. He's fourteen now, and fabulous!" He led her away from the clamor on stage, eager for a normal conversation.

"Are you working, or are you a stay-at-home mom, or doing both?" he asked, hoping the mom thing didn't offend her. It was hard telling where a woman's priorities were these days... so much had changed.

"Oh, yeah, still in the work-a-day-world. Once you dive into the pond of corporate finance it's difficult to swim your way out, it's got a strong undertow." Amanda leaned her back against the wall, flawlessly recreating their first encounter in the courtyard near the English wing so many years ago. "The last big market dip was a little stressful," she said, as she stirred her drink, "and I thought of quitting then, but I guess I'm just a glutton for punishment. Besides, I'm a little too Type A to be content playing wife and mother and doing nothing else. Don't get me wrong," she said, reaching out to touch Matthew's arm. "I love my husband and my son, but they're not the be-all and end-all, you know; a girl's got to have more than just home and family. Travel and nannies don't come cheap," she said dismissively as she took another sip of her drink. "What've you been up to?"

"I bounced around a little here and there after college. I spent a few years backpacking over Europe, and I ran a restaurant with a guy I met in Paris. It failed miserably – I lost a ton on that deal – but I learned a lot. There were a couple of lean years there, but I pulled it out of the fire before getting my short hairs singed," he said with a wry grin that he hoped would mask his disappointment at his own failure. "I spent some time designing websites until code manipulation became drop and drag easy, and the bottom fell out." He took a sip of his drink and looked around the room, hoping Jason would rescue him; but that guy was nowhere in sight, as usual. Matthew looked at Amanda, trying to discover if she wanted to hear more or if he could easily escape. She did, and he couldn't. "Now, I've got a three-hundred square foot tiny cabin near a small lake, and I'm working with a non-profit training dogs to support veterans with PTSD. I love the work. It doesn't pay a lot, but it's very rewarding, and working with dogs all day – you just can't beat that!"

"I suppose…" Amanda replied, absently teasing the ice cubes in her glass with the swizzle stick and scanning the room.

Matthew was uncomfortable, and she felt it too. It was clear that their lives had traveled in different directions and they were now two people who had little in common. The band forced their exit – although it wasn't the departure either were hoping for. A spotlight fell on the pair. Their embarrassment radiated to the parking lot.

"There they are, folks, Matthew and Amanda, your homecoming King and Queen! Let's give them a big round of applause! And since they just happen to be standing together… how about a dance, you two, for old time's sake?!" The emcee was the same annoying kid he was at the school talent shows, that much hadn't changed. The pair tried to beg off, but he wouldn't have it. "Come on, you two... let's relive our glory days!"

The crowd cheered and clapped, as the first few bars of a poorly conceived Springsteen tribute erupted from the stage. Matthew and Amanda knew there was no way to get out of it. The music began, and the sea of people parted as they walked to the center of the dance floor. It was the same music from the old days, but there had been too much distance, too much time... the strong emotions that once lived so exuberantly were now lost to the past. When the music stopped, Matthew kissed Amanda on the cheek, and they retreated in separate directions; Amanda to find her husband and Matthew to find the bar.

****

Three years later, Matthew saw Amanda's obituary in the online version of their local newspaper. A particularly malicious form of cancer had ravaged her brain and caused a slow, agonizing death. He went to the funeral to pay his respects to the girl he'd once known and to the woman with whom he sadly, couldn't establish a connection.

Standing alone at the graveside, a young man who stood about six-foot-tall, with a slender build, and blue eyes tapped him on the shoulder. Matthew turned, and the young man said, "My mom wanted you to have this." He handed Matthew an envelope with a single sheet of paper folded inside. Mathew's face was drawn up in a question mark. "Mom gave me a photo from your reunion, that's how I knew who you were."

Matthew opened the letter to discover a lab report originating several years ago, from the same place where he'd donated his sperm during those lean years. On the bottom left corner, a note read, "I always loved you, but was too chicken to make it real. This was as close as I could do. Sorry, Amanda."

Matthew looked up from the letter, mute and astonished, at the young man standing before him.

"Good to finally meet you, Dad," the teen said with a gentle smile. "I'm Christopher."

Club 13

"Hello, Linda? Hi, this is Susan."

"Hi, Susan! It's great to hear from you. How was your vacation?"

"Utah was wonderful, we had a fabulous time. Sorry I haven't called sooner; we got back a week ago, and we've just been regrouping, getting ourselves back into normal life; you know how challenging that can be, checking in with the boys at college and doing laundry," Susan said with a bit of exhaustion in her voice.

"Of course," said Linda. "No worries, I knew we'd catch up again when you had the time."

"Say, Linda, sorry to bother you at work, but the reason I was calling... are you and Richard free for dinner tonight? It would be great to hang out with both of you again, and we'd love to tell you about our trip."

"Absolutely, Susan! What time would you like us?" asked Linda.

"How does seven o'clock sound? That'll give Mark a little time to decompress from work before dinner."

"Sounds great, what can I bring?" asked Linda with a knowing hint in her voice.

"How about dessert... something chocolate?" Susan giggled.

"I knew you were going to say that! This'll be fun. I can't wait to see you."

"Me too, have a great afternoon."

"You too, bye."

"Bye."

****

The two couples had a relaxing dinner and dessert. Afterward, they took their coffee into the living room and talked a little bit about Susan and Mark's Utah vacation. Mark pulled out a brochure for *Club 13* and handed it to Richard.

"What's this? You trying to recruit us to the dark side, Mark?" Richard said with a snicker.

"Something like that," laughed Mark. "Look, this is a really cool program, and our membership is almost up," he said, looking toward Susan. "The rules don't allow us to renew for a while... you know, to give others a chance – it's a limited membership, very exclusive – so we wanted to talk with you two, and see if you'd be interested in taking the transfer on our slot… with the understanding, of course, that we get it back when yours expires," said Mark.

"What's this all about, Susan?" asked Linda. "I thought this was just your average timeshare thing, like Disney. Now you're saying it's different than that? I'm not sure I understand."

"It is *much* different. But it's nothing perverse, Linda," Susan said with a laugh. "It's just a little bit hard to explain. We'll tell you everything, but you've got to promise to keep an open mind."

Linda looked at Richard, taking a sip of her coffee, wary of this new side of their friends they'd not seen before. They seemed so serious. Richard nodded his agreement about the unspoken weirdness that hung in the room, put the brochure on the table and said, "Alright Mark, what's this all about?"

"I'll try to explain it as best I can. I promise, it's nothing scary, illegal, or immoral. Just keep an open mind, okay?" Mark asked.

Linda's eyes held hope that their friends would accept easily what they were about to hear.

"Okay," Richard and Linda agreed hesitantly.

"There's a myth," began Mark, "within the hospitality industry that it's bad luck to include a room or a floor with the number thirteen in your hotel."

"Sure," said Linda. "We've heard that before... an old wives tale some contractors made up, like don't walk under a ladder."

"That's only part of it," said Susan.

"Few people know how the myth actually began," said Mark. "In the mid-1800s, after decades of mysterious deaths, unexplained accidents, and thousands in lost revenue, the Board of Directors of the International Hotel Consortium held a meeting to try to find the culprit and a solution. After months of discussion, they decided that the negative encounters their visitors were having at their hotels were because the number thirteen was included on their floor plans. Everyone knew the number thirteen was bad luck, and they thought that if they simply eliminated that number from their floor plans, and just leave rooms twelve and fourteen with the gap in the numbering sequence, superstition would be appeased, and the bad luck could be avoided."

"However," continued Susan, "the number of incidents increased, rather than declined." She looked to Mark for confirmation. He concurred, and she continued. "They were at a loss about what to do when, one day, at one of their board meetings in the 1890s, one of the Consortium members suggested that they consult with a local spiritualist to help find a solution."

"Spiritualists? You mean like that stuff Houdini was trying to debunk... Ouija boards and séances ... that kind of stuff?" asked Linda.

"Exactly," replied Susan. "That stuff was really big at the time, lots of people believed in it. Anyway, when they consulted the spiritualist, they discovered that Hecate, the Greek Goddess of Crossroads, who protects travelers from evil on the road, was angry because room thirteen was being ignored. There are a lot of places in antiquity where the thirteenth of a group appears as the most powerful and the most sublime. Out of this anger of a power being ignored, Hecate was exacting revenge on those who were staying in rooms twelve and fourteen or staying in rooms on the twelfth and fourteenth floors."

"The spiritualist," Mark continued, "held a séance and made a pact with Hecate that if the hotel developers promised to build a special hotel catering only to room thirteen, the trouble would stop. Hecate agreed, but demanded that there must be at least one hotel of this nature built in each of the United States, and at least one in every country in the world, to appease her and revere the number thirteen properly."

Richard and Linda were dumbstruck. They'd never known their friends to hold any religious beliefs. In fact, they both thought that Mark and Susan were atheists. In all the years they'd been friends, through raising their children together, camping trips, and backyard parties, they'd never realized that the couple had any inclination of religion, let alone held any beliefs in ancient spirituality.

"So, I'm confused. How does this all connect to us and the timeshare?" asked Richard.

"Well, this is how *Club 13* was created," said Susan, indicating the brochure in front of the couple. "Each time a new hotel chain is built, a floor is constructed in a separate building, away from *normal* travelers. It's a special hotel that is blessed according to the pact made with Hecate. This is how they appeased her back then, and the practice is still going on today. It's kind of like the Masons... a secret society that goes back hundreds of years... only this is specifically about hotels."

"Only the truly adventurous become members," added Mark. "You never know exactly what your vacation will look like until you get there. Once you're a member, you can travel all over the world and stay in any *Club 13* that you want. Each visit must last thirteen days, and each resort is connected in some way to either an astrological or geological reference point to the number thirteen. No one knows exactly where they're going until they arrive within thirteen hundred miles of the particular

Club 13 where they will be staying."

Susan nodded excitedly, as she finished her coffee. "Also, members can't travel to any *Club 13* location more than once... which is perfectly okay, they have a lot of them, and in some pretty exotic locations, too!" Linda and Richard could tell that Susan was hooked on this vacation plan. When she talked about it, her face lit up as if she were a small child talking about her recent trip to The Magic Kingdom.

"Membership dues are $13,000 per year, and you can take up to three trips a year. Of course, air and land travel to get to the resort are separate. There can only be thirteen thousand registered members of *Club 13* at any given time, worldwide," explained Mark.

"Is that individual members, or registered families?" asked Richard. He could feel himself getting genuinely sucked into the myth and the sales pitch.

Linda was still confused. She could find no words and was having a tough time wrapping her brain around what this all meant.

"Each family is considered a registered member. But it's only immediate family, just parents and children. Extended family like grandparents, aunts and uncles, cousins, or nieces and nephews and grandchildren aren't included. It's strictly forbidden to discuss *Club 13* with them, or your friends... unless your membership is due to expire, and you want to recruit them; like we're doing with you," said Susan with a motherly smile. "That's why we haven't really talked about our vacations with you in any detail until now."

Linda simply said, "Uh, okay." She looked at Richard for some reassurance, but he was no help. He was focused on Mark and the sales pitch.

"Membership expires after thirteen years and cannot be renewed again until another thirteen years have elapsed." Mark went on as if he were selling Richard a lease for a new car. Susan was right there with them, nodding encouragement. "Members in their thirteenth-year recruit others to become members.

"It's really important," Susan added, "for outgoing members to recruit replacements because the way the pact was struck with Hecate, if the membership numbers fall below the required thirteen hundred she has the option to declare the pact null and void, and she can go back to wreaking havoc again, indefinitely."

"So far," added Mark, knocking on the wood of the coffee table, "that hasn't happened."

"I'm a little confused... just what makes this timeshare so special? How is this Greek goddess, what's her name..." asked Linda.

"Hecate," interjected Susan.

"Right, Hecate... just how is it that the *international* hotel industry is keeping her happy?" Linda's face screwed up with utter bewilderment. Susan took pity on her and poured her another cup of coffee to ease her mind.

"Yes, that's an interesting point," added Richard. "How *does* that work?"

Susan was pleased that finally, Richard seemed to be misunderstanding, too. It made her feel a little inept to think she was the only one who didn't get it.

"Well, each *Club 13*... remember, there's at least one in each state... has a floor dedicated to all the room thirteens of a particular chain, kind of like a tribute hotel; or a penance hotel, if you like." Mark explained. "For instance, one floor would be devoted to Holiday Inn, one for Comfort Inn Suites, one for Best Western, and another for Embassy Suites. There are others, but those are the big four. Each *Club 13* has only thirteen floors. If there are more hotel chains to dedicate than thirteen, a separate *Club 13* resort is built next door or on another plot of land in the same state. More resort buildings are added as hotel chains are created; and as hotels go out of business, floors are rededicated."

"There's a big ceremony and everything!" exclaimed Susan. "It's really exciting."

"They must have invested in a lot of property, early on," said Richard.

"Yes, they did. Land was a lot less expensive back then, and they stocked up, keeping a seven… or in this case… a thirteen-generation view of their future," Mark chuckled.

"Each floor for each dedicated hotel chain has a theme, and each floor has, as you might imagine, only thirteen rooms." Susan began to tick the items off on her fingers, repeating each hand as she ran out of fingers. "The **Holiday Inn** rooms are thematic to each of the major holidays for a particular country. For the U.S. that would include Christmas, Easter, Halloween, Thanksgiving, New Year's Eve, Valentine's Day, St. Patrick's Day, and some others.

"The **Comfort Inn Suites** rooms focus on comforting moments, things, and activities. You know, stuff like massages and hot baths, bedtime storytelling, home-cooked or specially prepared meals by a 'grandmother' figure, and baby animals." Susan's smile was so big, and her voice so wistful, Linda was certain she was reliving her memory of snuggling with cute baby animals on one of their timeshare trips.

Mark picked up where she left off, as he could clearly see that Susan was lost in a sea of soft, cozy memories. He shot her a quick smile and continued. "The thirteen rooms for the **Best Western** chain get you involved in various western scenes and situations like shootouts, cattle drives, saloon poker games, bank robberies, wagon trains, pony express deliveries, and gold mining.

"The **Embassy Suites** floors have rooms that celebrate a day-in-the-life of various countries wherever the USA has an embassy. France, England, Spain, Canada, Japan, Egypt, Germany, Brazil, Australia, Rome, and sometimes others, depending on where you are in the world. They expose you to a bunch of situations and events like food, decorations, costumes, local celebrations, all that stuff; a different country every day. It's kind of like traveling abroad without the requirement of a passport." Mark chuckled, this was his favorite of the membership perks.

"So, let me get this straight," said Richard, glancing over at Linda to be sure she was following along. "For $13,000 a year, for thirteen years, you can take up to three, all-inclusive, thirteen-day trips, every year, to resorts all over the world that provide unique experiences that you probably can't get at any other vacation resort anywhere else in the world, and you'll never be overwhelmed by crowds and delays in service or broken toilets, and we can take both kids, and the only catch is that we can't talk about the membership specifics or give away the locations to people who aren't members?"

"Yup. That's about it," said Mark.

Susan smiled and nodded in agreement. "Oh, and you have to promise to recruit us back when your term expires."

"In thirteen years," reminded Linda with an understanding grin.

"Yes," said Susan, pleased that Linda was finally on the same page.

"That works out to..." Richard looked to the ceiling as he did the math on the imaginary calculator that hung from the joists. "...just over four grand per trip for four people?"

"Yup," said Susan.

"That's cheaper than Disney," Richard said as he looked at Linda.

"Yup," Mark and Susan said in unison.

Linda and Richard locked eyes and inhaled deeply. Anyone not privy to the conversation would have thought they were practicing Lamaze. A beat later, they turned back simultaneously and said,

"Sign us up!"

Richard and Mark shook hands. Susan and Linda hugged.

"Oh good," Susan squealed, "now I can show you pictures from Utah! We stayed on a Best Western floor." She jumped up to put on another pot of coffee. "You're going to love this!"

Business as Unusual

Things here aren't as wonderful as you might think. Following your husband to his business posting is much like being a military wife – you go where they send you and you don't ask too many questions. It's not really all that bad here, a little drab, maybe. I do miss the colors of home, though. Looking at it all through the portal is less heartwarming than basking in its glow without barriers.

I don't get out much, the weather is so fickle, and in my delicate condition, it's better just to stay indoors. Besides, it's cold most of the time, and the rest of the time it's too dark to feel safe. It's an alien place – and you never know who or what will be lurking about the streets. The baby is due soon, and I'd rather not take any chances. John feels more comfortable with me staying close to home, too. We're right around the corner from the medical clinic, and he's always been the pragmatic one when it comes to spending as little time in a panicked state as possible. John has firmly concluded that he will be panicked the day I go into labor. I think it's good that he's planning ahead, it reduces the suspense.

I haven't looked for work yet. I don't think anyone would hire me right now, and besides, John and I made an agreement that I'd stay home with the baby full time – we both think that's best, but I must admit, until he's born, I'm bored... a lot. What I wouldn't give for something new to do – even taking a crack at my mother-in-law's recipe book would be better than just sitting around doing nothing all the time... but John packed the books, and I've no idea where it is.

Don't get me wrong... I'm not complaining... being a housewife is a noble choice. I'm proud to stay at home and do what I can to support my husband and help prepare for our impending family. It's taken us a long time to get here, and now, comfortably, we are walking forward into a future that is both uncertain and exciting. I just wish he'd be more help in clearing out the basement.

I'm nesting, I know... it's hormonal. It's also normal; at least that's what I tell John. But from where he sits, the word 'normal' is an oxymoron.

We talked about decluttering and agreed we'd tackle it before having children to make room for the new baby, both physically and emotionally. It's been almost two years since he accepted the transfer, and still, boxes remain filled with the memories and mess of the past. Most of it is not mine.

I realize he's busy with his career, but so much of what's down there, I'm not qualified to make decisions about what to keep and what to toss, simply because it's NOT MY STUFF! Not to mention the fact that I know he'd become irritated if I did it without him. But the truth remains, I can't ignore it any longer. I've got to do something before I explode into the wifezilla he never wanted. Either I take on the challenge of going through the mountain of boxes, or he takes on the challenge of dealing with me in a psychotic state as fallout for not dealing with the clutter. We've only got four months left... there's no more time to "get to it later."

So, finally, this afternoon, in an earnest effort to locate the fabled "Mom's Recipe Book" and give me something new to occupy my time while John was out on his moonwalk collecting rocks, or performing some obscure scientific research, I ventured into the basement to see what could be done. The room was dank and dismal, as most basements are, but I wasn't bothered... too much. There was a modicum of light seeping in through the tiny windows just above ground level. It wasn't enough. I pushed the small electric panel on the wall next to the door and illuminated the room with fluorescent wonderment.

As I looked around the space, I evaluated the job before me. To my left were several boxes marked "new house-keep," in my handwriting. I can't quite remember what's in them, but I decided to look through those boxes last. Since they'd already been marked as "keep" and in my handwriting, I knew the book wasn't in there. So, half the decision had been made regarding that stack, at least. As my father always said, "If you do the longer, harder tasks first, you'll accomplish more in the long run." My father lived well into his nineties, so who was I to discount his advice? I moved on to another stack.

I looked to my right. In the corner stood a stainless steel, commercial freezer. It was wide enough and deep enough to hold a dead body, but short enough that one probably wouldn't fit. I decided to clean it out later. John packed it before we left, saying that he didn't want to waste any food. "Culinary delicacies are a rare commodity up there," he'd said. "I don't want to have to live without eating the things I enjoy."

It made sense. After all, I'd been craving Moose Tracks ice cream these past few weeks of my pregnancy. We didn't have much of it left, and I was beginning to become concerned we wouldn't get any more. So, his logic about keeping the stuff in the freezer made sense. There was plenty of room in the kitchen freezer for whatever he'd packed, so I knew we could move it upstairs later. Truth be told, if it were up to me, I'd get rid of the old thing, it makes a loud humming noise that is beyond irritating, and the sound echoes up from the basement whenever I'm trying to read or sleep – it's very bothersome. Two stacks done.

Just then, a storm hit our area, and sunspot lightning came rushing through the window slits enveloping the basement in an orange strobe effect reminiscent of my teenage years at the high school dance when I got an evil migraine while everyone else got wicked drunk. I prayed that the storm would pass quickly. They usually do, but you can never tell. So, I crouched on the floor and started going through the stacks closest to me, hiding behind a tower of boxes that shielded me from the window's glare.

Over the next two hours I ravaged a myriad of boxes, pulling a lot of things out, putting most of them back in, and marking the box "trash" in gigantic red letters with my favorite Sharpie. There was nothing of consequence, nothing John would miss, I was certain of it. *After all, if he hasn't come to retrieve them during the past two years that we've been on this God-forsaken grey rock, he most likely never will.* I felt confident that they could be easily pushed the fifteen feet into the incinerator – with nary a whisper of discontent from John. Stack number three was done, and after the brief slide into the furnace, was heating the house with a warm glow.

I heard John's voice from the living room a few moments later.

"Julie, where are you?" he called.

"In the basement," I yelled.

"What on Earth are you doing down here?" he questioned, descending the stairs, skipping every other step.

"What on Earth? Funny," I chided. "I'm sorry, I just couldn't deal with the clutter any longer – I had to get rid of some of this junk."

John's amber eyes looked back at me with compassion and understanding. "I know, this stuff's been sitting for a long time, and I've been ignoring it for too long. I know I promised to help – I'm here now, what can I do?" he asked, with a warm embrace.

"Well, I think I've got the bulk of it taken care of... if you could just help me move the food from the freezer to the kitchen, I think we can let the rest go for a while," I suggested.

"Sure, I'd be happy to help," John said, a broad smile on his face.

As John opened the freezer, I watched as he began to pull various clear, plastic packages out and put them in a carryall to go upstairs. I couldn't figure out what kind of food it was, and so, being the forever curious soul, I walked a few steps closer to get a better look.

"John... are those ears... and is that a tail... f-fu-fur... W-wh-what is that?" came the squeak from my throat.

"Frozen dog!" he said, with a wistful sigh and a delighted grin.

"DOG?!" I hollered. "That's what's been sitting in our freezer for the past two years? That's the 'food' you didn't want to waste?"

"Well, yeah, what did you expect, alligator?" The scales on his face and neck rippled in disgust.

The Holiday Market

It was three days until Winter Solstice, and Sean was pleased with having crossed nearly everyone off his list. The last gift to buy was for his wife, Sophie. They'd been together fifteen years and still, he struggled with a gift that would make an impression. It wasn't so much that she was difficult to buy for, it was more that she enjoyed simple tastes, and sometimes those were difficult for merchants to price. She was easy to please... one glass of wine at dinner, chocolate chip cookies whenever she needed to celebrate, and a soft, small dog to cuddle when he was away on business. They rarely argued and shared a love of children. Even though Odin hadn't seen fit to bless them with a child yet, Sophie never lost hope that one day, he would.

Sean walked the aisles of the Holiday Market, hosted by the local Lion's Club, searching for something that couldn't be found in the shopping malls and high-priced boutiques. After so many seasons together, he knew the gift had to be special, a real stand-out, and he knew he wouldn't find that at some franchisee.

After passing rows of tables containing displays of hand-made quilts, hand-blown glass, beeswax candles, and the like, he was beginning to become discouraged. Although each item was unique and crafted with love, nothing he discovered was distinctive enough to match Sophie's delicate nature.

He was all but ready to leave when a diminutive elderly woman with bright hazel eyes caught his attention. She sat at the end of the last aisle, behind a table adorned with a red and gold tartan tablecloth and several small, hand-crafted wooded boxes in front of her. The boxes were beautifully carved, lacquered and finished to a polished sheen. The woman sat quietly sipping tea and stroking a tabby cat that sat upon a green cushion on a nearby chair. She wore a rough woolen coat and gloves without fingers.

"Is there something I can help you find, dear?" she asked gently.

"I'm searching for a Solstice gift for my wife. She loves unique presents, and beautiful things... I saw your lovely boxes and thought that it might be the perfect choice. How much are these?"

"The cost of the boxes is very inexpensive," she said. "Yet, what's inside... well, that son, is quite a bit more significant." She gave him a wry smile and her eyes twinkled as she took another sip of her tea.

"Really?" Sean asked, his curiosity piqued. "What do you have hiding inside?" He moved to pick up a box and open it, but she gently slapped his hand away before he could get the chance.

"Oh, you mustn't fondle the merchandise, dear. You might upset the gift, and that could be disastrous. These are special gifts and must be handled with the utmost care and concern," she tutted.

Sean was shocked, and now, even more curious by the old woman's words and actions. She was more agile that he'd imagined, even as her fingers were crooked with the effects of arthritis. "These boxes are indeed lovely," he said. "But what could they possibly hold that could be so delicate. I see you don't have signs..."

"We don't need signs," she interrupted, stroking the sleeping cat. "The gift you need is inside the right box, and there's never any confusion if it's the right one for you. Look them over carefully, hold the image of your wife... her heart, her soul, her dreams, in your imagination, and you will know which box holds the right gift for her."

Sean looked at her questioningly. When he set out that morning, he wasn't anticipating stumbling upon an old gypsy soul... but that's exactly what she seemed to be. It made him a bit wary and a bit amused, simultaneously. *Well, this is weird. She must be going senile. I'll just play along and give the old woman a little holiday money. No harm done.* He stuffed his hands in his pockets and regarded the boxes carefully. They sat in a haphazard collection, no specific display intention... yet beautifully presented. There were squares, trapezoids, octagons, rectangles, circles, stars... every shape you could imagine. Each was made of inlaid teak of every shade of the tree rainbow.

He thought about his dear Sophie and how she would be captivated by this old woman, her cat, and the conundrum he now faced. He could hear her say, "This is so much fun! Would you ever imagine this would happen to us! Which box should we choose?" She had the pure heart of a child, untarnished by the negativity that surrounded her daily life as an oncology nurse. Even though Sophie experienced so much pain and death every day, she never allowed it to diminish her love for life or her optimism for what the future would hold. Often, he wished he had her outlook and perseverance. Too often, he allowed his frustration to get the better of him. He felt like an incompetent husband because he couldn't give her a child – the one thing in life she wanted more than anything else. He would have given anything, including his own life, to make that dream come true for her, and there were times when he was annoyed with Odin for refusing her such a gift.

Sean continued to study the boxes, unsure of which to choose. The old woman noticed his apprehension and tried to help him along. "Don't take too long, dear. You don't want the gift to grow stale. You must be careful with your choice, but don't over-think it. Life offers up consequences for those who ask too much and delay the inevitable."

Stirred out of his musings by the old woman's comment, he selected a box. "I believe I'll take this one," he said, pointing at an octagonal box with an alternating pattern of three shades of teak.

"A marvelous choice," the old woman crooned. "That'll be twenty dollars." She carefully wrapped the box in white tissue paper and gently placed it inside a red velvet drawstring bag as he retrieved the money from his wallet.

"Thank you very much," Sean said, gently laying the money in her creased and crooked hands. "I'm sure my wife will adore it."

"'Tis certain she will, young man. Remember, do not give it to her until Solstice night, else the gift will not have time to mature. In the meantime, cradle it carefully and after she opens it, help her to care for it."

"I promise I will," he said.

"Be certain, young man. Such a promise should not be hastily made." The old woman was sincere in her instruction, and he could not avoid her gaze.

"I promise," Sean said again, in full earnest and with a broad smile.

"Very well," she said, and handed him the package. "Happy Solstice."

"Thank you, Happy Solstice to you, and to your cat." At this the cat looked up and blinked. The old woman stroked its back. Contented that its presence had been acknowledged, it laid its head down and went back to sleep.

Three nights later, as Sophie and Sean sat together enjoying their festive meal on the soft carpet near the stone hearth of their old farmhouse, he presented her with the delicate bag.

"What's this?" she asked, a gentle smile on her face.

"Happy Solstice," he said.

"But we agreed we wouldn't buy each other gifts this year," Sophie said with a playful agitation in her voice.

"I know," Sean said. "But I saw this, and the old gypsy woman who I bought it from was certain you'd enjoy it."

"Gypsy woman? Where?" she asked.

"At the Holiday Market in the Square. Oh, you would have loved her." Sean's eyes lit up as he remembered the encounter. "She was terrific. She made me promise to take special care of this gift and only give it to you on Solstice night. She claimed that if I didn't, the gift wouldn't have time to mature. She had a cute cat, too."

"What's inside?" Sophie asked.

"I don't know," Sean replied.

"What do you mean, you don't know? You bought it for me, right?" She was puzzled by the whole affair. Although she loved surprises, in her line of work, she rarely encountered them. So much in the cancer world was predetermined and even though each individual's illness was different, it usually led down the same path. There was little room for deviation where outcomes were concerned.

"I don't know what's inside... she made me promise not to open it, but she said that if I waited, she was sure it would be the right gift for you. You would have loved her, Sophie; she was a distinctive soul. I went back yesterday, to see if I could find her again and maybe buy another box, but the director of the market said that she'd done what she came to do and has moved on. I'm not sure what that means, except that we probably won't be able to find her. The director said she paid cash for her table." Sean returned Sophie's puzzled gaze and added his own inimitable smile.

Sophie remained a little dumbfounded, still holding the gift in her hands, silent and still.

"Well, are you going to open it?" he asked with a smirk.

"I... I guess so," she said. Slowly and carefully she untied the drawstring and reached into the pouch. She pulled out the tissue-wrapped box and tilted her head at her husband, smiling again.

"Keep going," he said with a nervous giggle. "The suspense is killing me."

She unwrapped the tissue and revealed the beautiful box. "Oh Sean, this looks really expensive. You shouldn't have..."

"Just open it, will you... I can hardly stand the anticipation!"

Carefully, Sophie lifted the lid of the octagon box. Inside was a small fortune cookie. Silently, she lifted the cookie. Sean nodded his encouragement. With one smooth, gentle movement, she broke the cookie in two. Sophie set the empty half back in the box and pulled a small slip of paper out of the other half, then set that part of the cookie back in the box as well.

"Odin is pleased with your love and patience," Sophie read aloud. "By Autumn Equinox you will receive the gift of life in triplicate, reflecting the strength, kindness, and love you share. Take care as you wait. Don't expect too much, and much will be given. Rush your heart and consequences will be yours to endure."

The two looked at each other, down at the tiny fortune, and back at each other again as a bemused, quiet excitement enveloped their souls. They hugged and kissed, each sharing tears as they delighted in the wonderment of the season.

Nine months later, at FallFest near the Autumn Equinox, three tiny souls, Ian, Megan, and Connor, made their Earthly debut amidst songs of praise to Odin and his promise of a life fulfilled.

Flying The Friendly Skies

In years past, whenever you traveled by air, your biggest concern was whether your luggage was too heavy. The airlines enforced strict weight limitations on aircraft, and if you exceeded those limits, they would need to onboard extra fuel to keep the aircraft flying, so you paid an extra fee. It all made perfect sense. The laws of gravity clearly stated that travelers were expected, if they wanted to arrive on time and in one piece at their destination, to obey the constraints of off-land travel. Although some people groused about the extra money spent to get to their vacation in Seattle, Vegas or Disney, no one ever cancelled their travel plans over it. It simply wasn't that big a deal.

Later, as our culture became more aware of turbulence, confined spaces, and the damage that could be done by personal choices that affect the comfort and well-being of others, new rules were established. To protect us from the tumult of unknown cloud formations and air patterns, seatbelts were made mandatory, as were flotation devices, and oxygen masks. Airlines quickly eliminated our right to poison our lungs at thirty-five-thousand feet. They also abolished the opportunity for two individuals to occupy a single lavatory or flight seat simultaneously. This last regulation curtailed considerably the fun-factor of flying, but again, these protocols didn't prohibit the vast majority from following through on their holiday plans.

This year, as I was preparing to travel to Oshkosh, Wisconsin for a business convention, I noticed a new addendum attached to my ticket voucher when I downloaded it. Evidently, travelers not only have to weigh their luggage and leave their wild ways at home, they must now agonize over the possibility that their baggage is too heavy. It seems the airlines have now instituted a punishing policy that requires passengers to declare their disposition, and if it's too arduous, they must check it and pay an extra fee to ensure that their baggage doesn't muck up the works; or if it does, appropriately compensate the airline for the nuisance.

The policy attached to my ticket reads, in part:

Passengers are permitted only tranquility, jocularity, conformity, sensitivity, and non-combative indifference in their carry-on. Contingent on the intensity, passengers may include a little stress, a smidge of depression, or perhaps a modest amount of anxiety, but beyond that, extra fees will be assessed without responsibility or liability on behalf of the airline. The standard measurements of "little," "smidge," and "modest" are at the sole discretion of the airline and the assigned ground and flight crew for a particular journey. Those passengers who suffer from aviophobia and have a valid reason from a medical professional for making the above-ground trip, will be permitted on board, but must show proof of properly prescribed medication to contain their angst.

Families flying with children are permitted a single carry-on per person, and supplementary tariffs will be assigned for children with oversized or unrestrained baggage. As they are still far too immature, infants under the age of two years are exempt from this policy. However, the airline strongly advises that families weigh carefully the necessity of flying with infants, and the irritation such a choice may cause. Childrens' baggage must be pushed deep into the overhead compartment. Tucking a child's baggage under the seat in front of the child will not be permitted, as it may become too accessible to the child, and may become dislodged during flight, disrupting the other passengers and flight crew. If a child's baggage doesn't fit, it must be checked into the cargo hold, and the family will be assessed the extra fine, payable before take-off. If a child surreptitiously brings contraband baggage onto the flight, parents or guardians are held solely responsible, and extra fees, as well as future bans to fly with this airline, may be levied.

Pilots and flight crew have dominion over the cabin, cockpit, galley, and lavatories from the moment the plane pushes away from the gate to the time it lands at its destination. Frenzies will not be tolerated. Flight crew have the right make the request, and pilots have the right to oblige a return of the aircraft to the airport of origin, and request that officials deplane any individuals discovered to be in non-compliance. Passengers will not be compensated in any way for delays or other annoyances for such a decision made by the pilot. Travelers who intermingle their excessive baggage with alcohol or pharmaceuticals, prescription or not, will be met at the gangway by sheriffs, and promptly escorted out of the terminal where they will be processed by Federal, State, or local TSA enforcement, and quite possibly fined, jailed, or both.

Please note that it is customary for the TSA to use baggage-detecting dogs to determine a passenger's compliance with this policy. If a dog targets a passenger as a possible violation or threat, that passenger will be removed from the boarding process and questioned by TSA officials. If this process exceeds the time necessary for a passenger to board their flight in a timely manner, passengers may be rerouted to another flight to their intended destination, and their luggage forwarded, if they are found not in violation. If, however, a passenger is found in violation of the baggage check policy, refunds or exchanges will not be provided, and local authorities will address the matter further.

After this new policy information, at the bottom of my ticket, there is a single line printed in bright magenta:

Thank you for ticketing your travel plans with our airline, and we hope you enjoy Flying The Friendly Skies.

Slimy Surprise

She hadn't prepared me for the airboat. Or the Neanderthal. All she said was, "This is the story you've been waiting for. Meet the guy at that place and tell him I sent you." That was it. Just a link to a Google map and the name "Ed." It was like a scene from the cutting room floor of a bad Bogart film. But, she'd never sent me a go-nowhere lead before, and because of her, I was living a comfortable life. So of course, I followed my phone's GPS and drove where she sent me.

If you've never been on one, an airboat is not much more than a flat piece of aluminum with a couple benches and a GIGANTIC airplane propeller on the back end of the thing. It doesn't look very stable, and at first glance, you wonder how all the lift from those blades doesn't send you immediately airborne. The seats were covered with brown canvas tarps.

Introductions with Ed was an interesting experience. He dressed in blue jean overalls, no shirt, and combat boots. His skin was scaly in some places, slimy in others. As he shook my hand, he said, "So you're the one LeeAnn sent? Are you sure I can trust you?" His voice had a strange croak to it.

Can I trust you? Is what I thought. What I said was, "Of course. LeeAnn would never steer either of us wrong, now would she?"

"I suppose not," he responded with a shrug. With that, and nothing more, he picked me up like a three-year-old and hoisted me off the dock and onto the airboat.

As the powerful engine first began to purr, and then grow into a roar, he pulled the boat out into the center of the waterway and skillfully sped toward the swamp. The dark, dismal, dank swamp. LeeAnn had warned me with a tidbit about a swamp being involved – after our failed five years together, she had at least walked away with the understanding that when it came to the abysmal in life, I wasn't a fan of surprises. But she'd told me nothing more than I would be traveling near a swamp. LeeAnn was a chronic under-explainer.

Not knowing what I was about to float into, I had my camera at the ready. I didn't know the purpose of this strange trip, the whys and the whats, but I accept that as part of the job. I promised not to take Ed's photo before he had a shower, but I couldn't resist sneaking just one. There was something in my gut that said it would be important later. Then I pointed my lens outside the boat and waited to arrive at our destination – wherever that might be.

I've been a freelance photojournalist for about ten years, avoiding corporate entanglements and only working when, where, and why I want to. It is a life I designed with purpose and laziness at the heart of it all. After five years working as a runner on Wall Street and socking away a ton of cash (insider information didn't come cheap), I got out as quickly as I could, before that world began to crash in on those who weren't paying attention.

I've been towing my tiny house around the United States, Mexico, and Canada, with little permanence ever since. No family and no obligations except the dog, a long-haired dachshund named Charlie, and my camera. Freelance photo jobs are not hard to come by in a world that no longer has the time or patience for words. Living off the grid lends me a kind of security unmatched by any other living situation I've ever known – including the years with LeeAnn – but that's another story.

I wasn't sure where this guy was taking me, I only knew that a connection through a mutual acquaintance of LeeAnn's told her that Ed could lead me to a story that would keep me in dog snacks and propane for the rest of my life. LeeAnn, still working at the money rat race, also still loved me enough to throw me a bone now and again, when she thought it might lead to something that would make me quit and come back to her. There was little chance that would ever happen. My life had become simple, and I was enjoying it. The only other piece of information was that there was some sort of mystery involved –

there always is when it's the Louisiana bayou – and I was assured this wouldn't be a waste of film. How could I possibly pass up a job like that?

Ed throttled the airboat back to a purr and pulled an 'S' maneuver through the Bald Cypress trees and quicksand-like mess that filled the area. Moss hung from the branches and an alligator slapped its tail and dove under the reeds as we drove past. My heart jumped, and my blood raced. Death by archaic carnivore was absolutely not my idea of a good time.

As we rounded the last curve, he coaxed the boat into a nearly imperceptible crawl. The bog was silent. I searched for a horizon, for a landmark, for anything that might hint at our location, but found none. I couldn't even see the sky through the dense overgrowth. Redundancy permeated the landscape, and, in that moment, I realized I was completely dependent on this near-Neanderthal stranger to get me back to Charlie. I've had more comforting thoughts.

A few seconds later, one word escaped Ed's throat; a guttural, unnatural noise; "Up."

I pointed my lens to the trees and started pressing the shutter even before my eyes could adjust to the shadows. Bodies hung from the trees like piñatas at a Cinco de Mayo party. Bones rattled together in the swamp breeze, a warning to defilers and deserters alike. The skeletons wore a skin of thick moss, brown and green, the stench of something beyond death seeping from every crevice.

"How long?" was all I could manage.

"A hundred fifty years," Ed replied.

I swallowed hard, regained my composure, and started doing my job. I touched the tiny voice recorder pinned furtively to my slicker's top clasp. "What happened here?" I asked, while pointing, shooting, and working hard not to eliminate the bile that threatened my restraint.

"No one knows for sure," he said, steadying the boat with a line looped precariously around a nearby empty tree limb. "But the story goes that some pirate made off with a load and left behind these guys to watch over it until he returned to fetch it. Never happened, though. The loot's still there."

I looked at him in utter disbelief. "And you know this how?"

"'Cuz I found it," he said flatly. "You don't think I'd drag a young lady such as yourself into 'gater land for nothing, do you? I ain't that desperate." His face cracked into a sly grin. "I was huntin' 'gaters out here a few weeks ago when my boat run aground; easy to do in this swamp, that's why the airboat, it's got almost no drag. Anyways, when I was workin' to get her out, I come upon this box, hardened like steel, the brass fittings still attached. Wasn't sure what I was lookin' at, so I marked it. I've seen your photos in that National Geographic magazine, and thought you might be a good one to prove my find. Then I got a buddy of mine to contact you, and here we are."

"You found a box? Where?" I'd been on treasure expeditions before and turned up zilch; photos of nothing don't make a great story, Geraldo Rivera can testify to that. I was reluctant to go all-in, or even half-in until I saw the thing. Now I understood why LeeAnn gave me so little information. Chances are, she was given little information. The mention of a hundred-and-fifty-year-old box at the bottom of a swamp before I'd met him at the dock would have kept me at home with Charlie, grilling cheeseburgers.

"Well, here's the thing. I'm not so sure I want to tell you..." Ed began.

"WHAT?" I interrupted. "You mean to tell me that you dragged my butt out of a warm bed for nonsense? There'd better be a hidden camera crew around here somewhere, or else you may have just found a way to swing in the breeze with those fellows up there!" I pulled out the Derringer Grandpa had given me, to make my point.

"Now, there's no need for that," he said, arms raised, one hand still holding the line for the boat. "I was just gonna say, I want to make sure you understand that before I show it to you, you gotta agree the find belongs to me, it's my story. I'll give you a small cut for your trouble, but nothing more; no byline except the photo credit. That friend of yours says you're a reasonable woman and you aren't too greedy... is that true?"

"That depends on what the find is, and how kindly you'll invest in me walking away," I said, repocketing the Derringer. "Everything's negotiable."

"Good enough" said Ed. He pulled us along, repositioning the tie-line about fifteen feet farther to a spot he marked with an alligator trap that had an extra loop around a second tree on its ballast end. In this place, it wouldn't have been suspect. It was a smart marker. Maybe he's not so Neanderthal after all. I put aside my camera and he handed me the spare shovel.

"What's this for?" I asked, stunned as he started to climb out of the boat with his own shovel.

"It's in there," he said, pointing to a place under the water at the root line of a huge Cypress.

"You mean we've got to dig it out?" LeeAnn said nothing about getting wet and muddy beyond description.

"What, you think after a hundred fifty years, it's just going to be sitting all nice and tidy on the bank, waiting for us?"

He had a point. I jumped in beside him, and we started to dig. We spent about two hours standing in murky, waist-deep water, digging the foot-locker-sized box out of the muck and mire of the swamp, all the while, watching for alligators and snakes. I'm not sure what unnerved me more, the sound of all those rattling bones, or the idea that at any moment, a cottonmouth would wrap itself around my leg and it, and the alligator, would fight over who got dinner first. Reptiles and I are not on speaking terms, even from a distance at the zoo. Every unaccounted-for ripple of the water sent waves of fear through me with the same intensity of the Wicked Witch on the Cowardly Lion.

Eventually, the box came loose with the thwack of muddy water sucking itself back into the hole. We hoisted it up onto the tarps, and after I climbed back into the boat I clipped off a few establishing shots. Ed reached a bailing bucket overboard and started to rinse the brass around the hatch and the lock. After several more photos and a slight shifting of the line tethering us to the tree, we looked carefully at the lock, examining how best to open it. He jimmied it here and there with a pair of needle-nose pliers, and I tried my hand at picking the lock with a six-inch length of extra radio wire. Neither had any effect.

After about twenty minutes, we'd both lost our patience, and without much fanfare, I pulled out the Derringer and blasted the lock. I'd like to say I was channeling Indiana Jones; but I didn't even come close. As hero-esque stuff goes, I was fairly pathetic. Yet, the tool did its job, and I reinforced my position as a woman who's not shy about firearms. That counted for points.

The lock shattered, as splintered wood flew from around the hatch. Ed pulled what was left of the lock off the box, and carefully opened it. Inside was every treasure hunter's dream. We grinned broadly at each other, and silently, carefully closed the box. After a few more photos, we got out of the swamp just as fast as we could. I'm not one to be superstitious, I don't believe in ghosts or curses; still, the whacking together of dangling skeletons certainly made for a compelling argument.

When we arrived back at the airboat hanger, after tying up, we hefted the box down the dock and back to his little shed. It was excrement-slimy, and so were we, covered in the sludge from the swamp, barely able to hold on to the thing. It jostled back and forth between his failing grip and mine. We nearly lost it entirely several times in the brief twenty-yard walk. *I hope Charlie doesn't mind the slime and stench... I hope it washes out of my clothes.*

****

The gold was Confederate and genuine, according an email exchange I received from LeeAnn and her contact in New York. I sent each of them a single shilling to secure an unbiased, scholarly opinion. After seeking out the professionals at a couple Ivy League institutions, they told us, "It's worth about ten grand cleaned up, more if there's a set of them." Of course, they wanted to know more, have more. Wall Street guys are like that. I told them they could keep it, which seemed to make them both happy – not delirious – but happy; and I told them nothing else. Except, I did tell LeeAnn that I was retiring and moving out of country. She was less than thrilled to learn that her plan had backfired, again. Nothing new there.

Ed kept his word and gave me sixty pieces of the gold and a nice photo-exposé in *NatGeo* for my trouble and snake anxiety. He kept the box, the jewels, the map in the bottle, and the glory, along with years of being hounded by the paparazzi and the academics.

Charlie got steak. I got lobster and we both relocated with our tiny house to a little swatch of beach in Panama. Even with everything, I'll take sand over slime every day – but I try to remember that a slimy surprise once bought me a new hat.

Drake, The Duck Muse

Drake has been Diana Kathryn's writing partner since she was seven years old. After decades of sitting on the sidelines and being content to quack story ideas and character development into her ear, he wanted to take a stab at writing his own collection of short stories. He is very grateful to Diana Kathryn for her typing skills. Feathers and keyboards don't always produce the best results.

Diana Kathryn Plopa is an author of five books (this book is her sixth, and her first collaboration). She is also the associate publisher and editor for Grey Wolfe Publishing, and the general manager of The Grey Wolfe Scriptorium bookshop in Clawson, Michigan. She loves nothing more than to spend hours listening to Drake quack and have fun with the stories and characters they create together.

Drake and Diana Kathryn enjoy life with her husband, Dave; their dogs, Alex and Finnigan; and spending time with her son, Zachary, and The Pack.

Cover Designer: Nafaa "Noofi" Makadsi

Noofi is an Iraqi-American artist, born in Baghdad, Iraq. Noofi spends his time drawing and breaking barriers associated with Down Syndrome.

When Noofi was three, he made his first drawing. It was a "portrait" of his grandmother. Since then, Noofi hasn't stopped drawing. Noofi loves using Prismacolor Markers, Spectra color Colored Pencils, and mixed media paper for his abstract work. Noofi wants to explore painting, charcoal, graphic design, and ceramics.

Noofi had two art shows at the YMCA North in Auburn Hills MI, and he was awarded for his achievements in breaking barriers with Down Syndrome, using his artwork from the Oakland County Community Mental Health Authority (Stigma Buster Award), and from the Friends of Community Living Services (Alice Saules Advocacy Award).

You can follow Noofi on his social media accounts, at **IAMNOOFI**.

Other Books by Diana Kathryn Plopa
(with Drake's guidance)

The Griffin of Greed (a children's fairy tale)
A Tryst of Fate (a thinking person's romance novel)
Free Will (a satirical novel about death)
Wolfe Cub (a memoir on single parenting)
Ideate Avail (poetry, currently out of print)

COMING SOON:
The Last Strand (a science fiction novel)
American Plague (a political thriller)
Splinters (a western novella)
The Scribe's Apprentice (an historical novella)

Learn more about Drake, the Duck Muse
and Diana Kathryn Plopa at
WWW.DKPWRITER.COM

Learn more about Grey Wolfe Publishing and
The Grey Wolfe Scriptorium at
WWW.GREYWOLFEPUBLISHING.COM

99049673R00061

Made in the USA
Columbia, SC
08 July 2018